UNITED STATES
NAVY
BY JOHN HAMILTON

VISIT US AT WWW.ABDOPUBLISHING.COM

Published by ABDO Publishing Company, 8000 West 78th Street, Suite 310, Edina, MN 55439. Copyright ©2012 by Abdo Consulting Group, Inc. International copyrights reserved in all countries. No part of this book may be reproduced in any form without written permission from the publisher. A&D Xtreme™ is a trademark and logo of ABDO Publishing Company.

Printed in the United States of America, North Mankato, Minnesota.
052011
042012

 PRINTED ON RECYCLED PAPER

Editor: Sue Hamilton
Graphic Design: Sue Hamilton
Cover Design: John Hamilton
Cover Photo: U.S. Navy
Interior Photos: AP-pgs 8-9; Thinkstock-pgs 5, 11, 13, 15, 19 & 25 (anchor, sailor & soldier silhouettes); U.S. Navy-pgs 1-7, 10-25, 27 (top), 28-32; U.S. Senate-pg 8 (John Paul Jones portrait); Wikimedia-Nate Voelker-pgs 26-27.

Library of Congress Cataloging-in-Publication Data

Hamilton, John, 1959-
  United States Navy / John Hamilton.
    p. cm. -- (United States Armed Forces)
  Includes index.
  Audience: Ages 8-15.
  ISBN 978-1-61783-071-6
  1. United States. Navy--Juvenile literature. 2. Warships--United States--Juvenile literature. I. Title.
  VA58.4H262 2012
  359.00973--dc23
                          2011020557

CONTENTS

THE UNITED STATES NAVY

Ships in the USS *Abraham Lincoln* Strike Group are led in a training exercise by the guided missile destroyer USS *Momsen*.

The United States Navy is the largest and most powerful navy in the world. It helps protect the nation from invasion, and keeps the oceans safe for shipping. It uses a combination of surface ships, aircraft, and submarines to fight wars in any part of the world.

The Navy's job is to preserve the peace and security of the United States. To accomplish its mission, it operates 286 ships and more than 3,700 aircraft. More than 400,000 active duty personnel and reserves keep the Navy afloat.

Three U.S. Navy ships, including an aircraft carrier, a guided-missile cruiser, and a guided-missile destroyer, sail to secure international waters.

A flight deck shooter signals an F/A-18 Super Hornet for takeoff.

Sailors provide protection for search-and-seizure teams in the Persian Gulf.

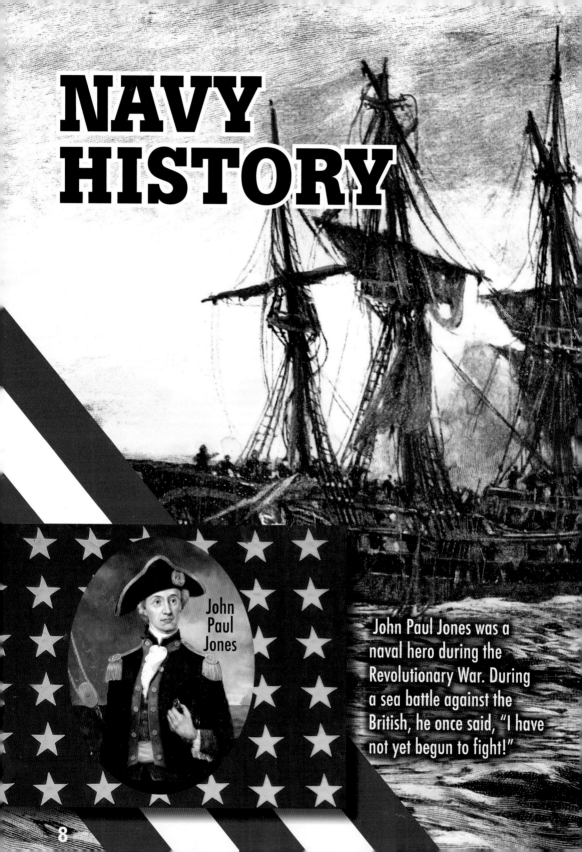

NAVY HISTORY

John
Paul
Jones

John Paul Jones was a naval hero during the Revolutionary War. During a sea battle against the British, he once said, "I have not yet begun to fight!"

John Paul Jones commanded the *Ranger*, an 18-gun sloop-of-war and one of the first ships in the American Continental Navy.

The Navy got its start during the Revolutionary War on October 13, 1775. Back then, it was called the Continental Navy. The Navy has fought in many wars, including the Civil War, World Wars I and II, Vietnam, Afghanistan, and Iraq.

NAVY TRAINING

A seaman recruit works at the radar station in the Command Information Center of the mine counter-measures ship USS *Defender*.

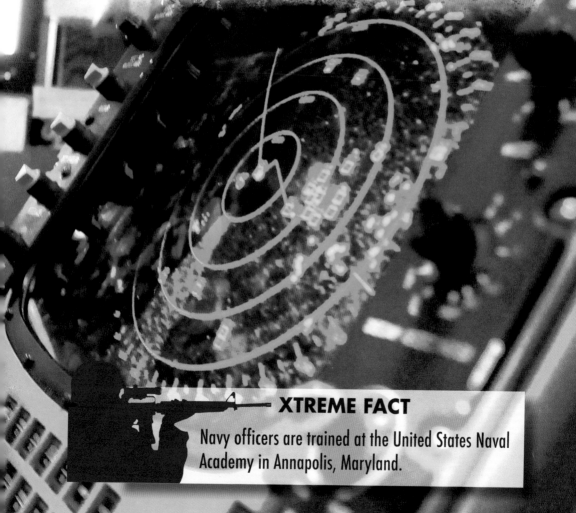

New members of the Navy are called seamen recruits. They must be at least 18 years old, with a high school diploma. Officer training usually requires a college degree. Recruits learn many naval warfare skills, including weapons training, aviation, electronics, engineering, and computers. When recruits finish their training, they are assigned to a ship or naval base.

XTREME FACT

Navy officers are trained at the United States Naval Academy in Annapolis, Maryland.

AIRCRAFT CARRIERS

A Sea Hawk helicopter parades the American flag over the aircraft carrier USS *Theodore Roosevelt*.

Some Navy ships, like gunboats, hold only a few people. Aircraft carriers are like floating cities. The USS *Theodore Roosevelt* is 1,092 feet (333 m) long. It carries nearly 6,000 people and 85 aircraft. Crewmembers nicknamed it "the Big Stick."

USS *Theodore Roosevelt*

XTREME FACT
Aircraft carriers don't sail alone. They are part of a group of support vessels called task forces, or battle groups.

NAVAL AIRCRAFT

The Navy extends its power with aircraft, which can strike targets far inland. The Navy uses fixed-wing aircraft and helicopters to attack the enemy and protect the fleet.

A Super Hornet launches from the USS *Ronald Reagan.*

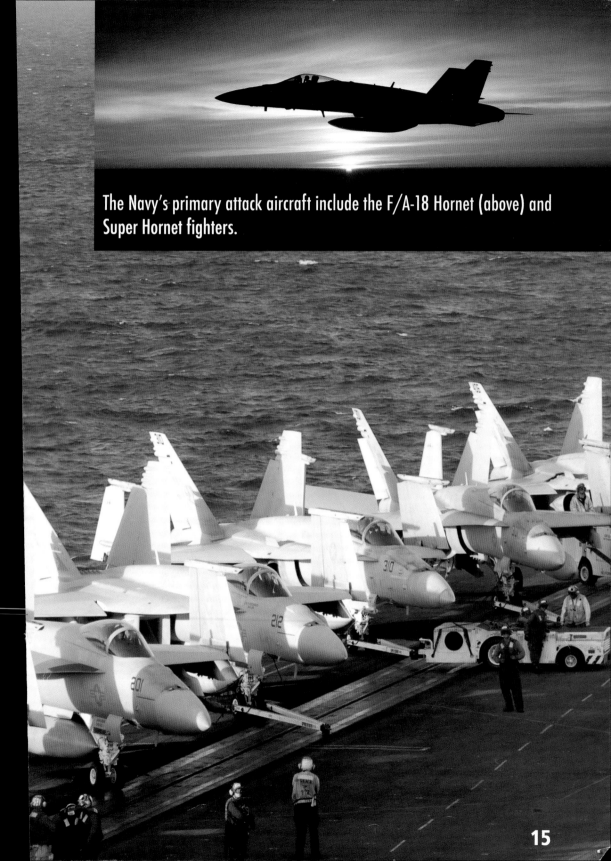

The Navy's primary attack aircraft include the F/A-18 Hornet (above) and Super Hornet fighters.

AMPHIBIOUS ASSAULT SHIPS

The Navy can land troops, usually U.S. Marines, on enemy shores by using amphibious assault ships. These vessels resemble small aircraft carriers, but use helicopters to support ground troops. Troops come ashore in LCAC hovercrafts. Amphibious assault ships also carry jets that can take off vertically, like AV-8B Harrier IIs.

An AV-8B Harrier II jet lands aboard the amphibious assault ship USS *Essex*.

A Landing Craft Air Cushion (LCAC) transports personnel and equipment.

CRUISERS

Cruisers are large vessels that can operate on their own or in battle groups. Many cruisers use the Aegis Combat System, powerful computer and radar systems that track and destroy enemy missiles or aircraft. Cruisers can also use Tomahawk missiles to strike at the enemy.

The guided-missile cruiser USS *Philippine Sea* conducts training operations in the Atlantic Ocean.

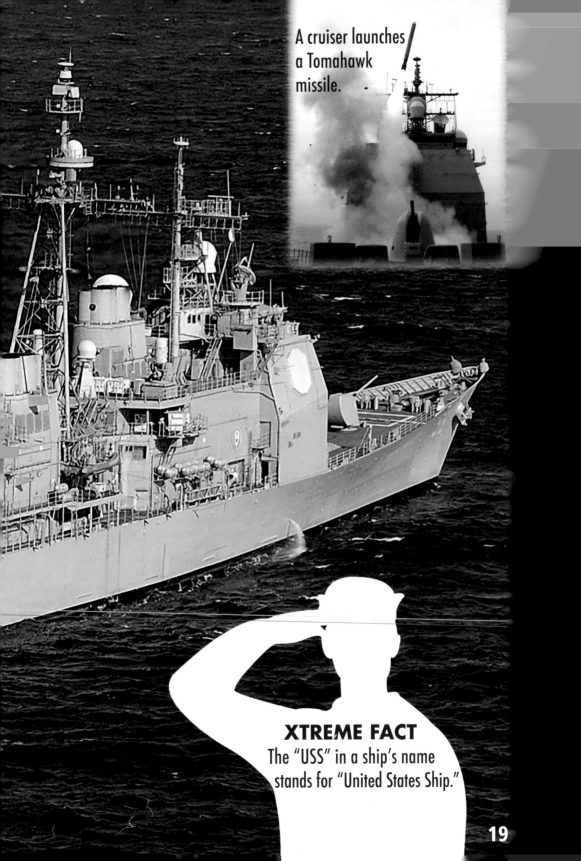

A cruiser launches a Tomahawk missile.

XTREME FACT
The "USS" in a ship's name stands for "United States Ship."

DESTROYERS

Destroyers are nicknamed "greyhounds of the sea." They are fast vessels that specialize in anti-ship and anti-submarine warfare. They can also strike offensively using Tomahawk cruise missiles.

XTREME FACT
Most destroyers are equipped with Sea Hawk helicopters to assist in fighting enemy submarines.

The guided-missile destroyer
USS *Mustin*.

FRIGATES

Frigates are smaller vessels that use torpedos and helicopters to protect Navy ships against submarines. They can also be used to intercept drug smugglers. Although frigates are limited in the missions they can perform, they are tough ships that can take a lot of damage.

A recoverable exercise torpedo is launched from the frigate USS *Klakring*.

The guided-missile frigate USS *Reuben James* deploys a search-and-seizure team off the coast of the Hawaiian Islands.

ATTACK SUBMARINES

Attack submarines detect and destroy enemy subs and surface ships. Armed with torpedoes and cruise missiles, they are quiet and fast. They can launch cruise missiles against land targets, and deploy special operations troops on enemy shores. The Navy has about 60 attack submarines in its fleet.

The Los Angeles-class attack submarine USS *Hampton* surfaces at the North Pole.

XTREME FACT

Most Navy attack submarines are Los Angeles-class vessels. They are 360 feet (110 m) long, with a crew of about 140.

BALLISTIC MISSILE SUBMARINES

The USS *Nevada* sails toward a port near Seattle, Washington.

Ohio-class ballistic missile submarines have one mission: to carry and launch Trident nuclear missiles, which can destroy entire cities. Ballistic submarines are nicknamed "boomers." They are bigger than attack submarines. The USS *Nevada* is 560 feet (171 m) long, with a crew of about 155. They can spend months underwater before firing up to 24 Trident missiles.

An unarmed Trident missile launches from the Ohio-class fleet ballistic missile submarine USS *Nevada*.

XTREME FACT
The Navy currently has 18 Ohio-class submarines in its fleet. Four of these have been converted to guided missile submarines, each of which can carry up to 154 Tomahawk cruise missiles.

THE FUTURE

A sailor mans the rails as the USS *Mason* departs for a six-month deployment.

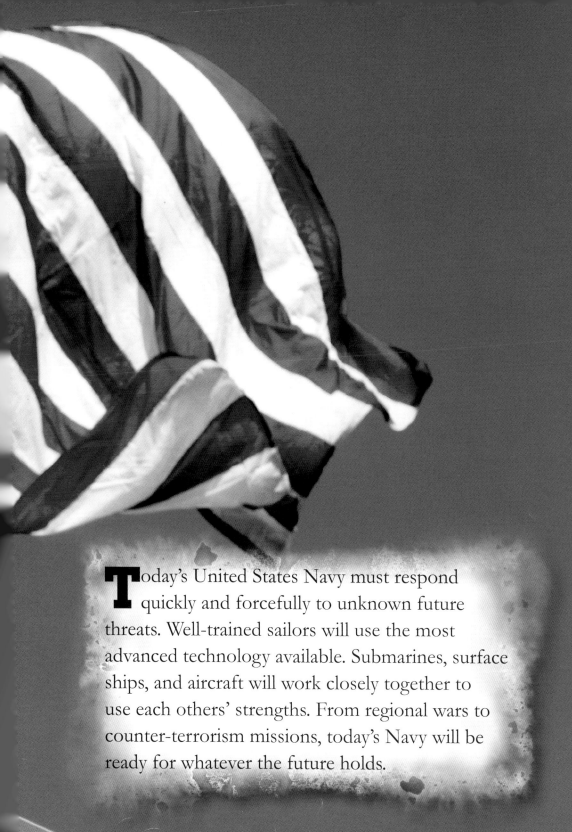

Today's United States Navy must respond quickly and forcefully to unknown future threats. Well-trained sailors will use the most advanced technology available. Submarines, surface ships, and aircraft will work closely together to use each others' strengths. From regional wars to counter-terrorism missions, today's Navy will be ready for whatever the future holds.

GLOSSARY

ACTIVE DUTY
People in the military who work full time in their jobs.

AMPHIBIOUS
Military operations that are launched from the sea against an enemy on water or land. Also, able to go on land or water.

BALLISTIC
An object, such as a ballistic missile, that begins with a powered upwards momentum, and then free-falls in a mathmatically-calculated path guided by gravity as it approaches its target.

DEPLOY
To move troops, ships, vehicles, and aircraft into position for military action.

FIXED-WING AIRCRAFT
A standard plane whose wings do not move, as opposed to an aircraft with movable wings, such as a helicopter.

FLIGHT DECK SHOOTER
A person who works on the flight deck of an aircraft carrier, signaling pilots to take off.

HOVERCRAFT
A vehicle that moves on land or water using a cushion of air.

RADAR
A way to find planes, ships and other objects. Radar stands for radio detection and ranging. The system sends out radio waves, which bounce off any objects they hit and reflect back to the source.

RESERVES
Military forces that are not on active duty, but can be called on to serve if needed by their country in an emergency.

TASK FORCE
A group of military forces brought together under one command for the purpose of conducting a specific task or goal. In the U.S. Navy, a task force may consist of an aircraft carrier, a cruiser, two destroyers or frigates, 65-70 aircraft, and about 7,500 personnel.

TOMAHAWK CRUISE MISSILE
A missile that can be launched from a submerged submarine, as well as a ship, or aircraft. It has stubby wings, and can be used over medium- to long-range distances.

INDEX